This book
belongs to

....

To Joe, with love

FREDERICK WARNE

Published by the Penguin Group
Penguin Books Ltd, 80 Strand, London WC2R oRL, England
Penguin Young Readers Group, 345 Hudson Street,
New York, New York 10014, U.S.A.
Penguin Books Australia Ltd, 250 Camberwell Road,
Camberwell, Victoria 3124, Australia
Canada, India, New Zealand, South Africa

2

ISBN-13: 978 07232 5905 3

Printed in Great Britain

Strawberry's New Friend

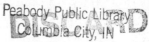
by Pippa Le Quesne

Welcome to the Flower Fairies Garden!

Where are the fairies?
Where can we find them?
We've seen the fairy-rings
They leave behind them!

Is it a secret
No one is telling?
Why, in your garden
Surely they're dwelling!

No need for journeying,
Seeking afar:
Where there are flowers,
There fairies are!

Contents

Chapter One
A New Friend

"Ouch!"

Strawberry pushed his way past the final bramble and emerged, very much the worse for wear, on the edge of a field.

"Ow, ow, ow!" he said, as he began to examine his injuries.

There were some painful scratches on his hands and arms and one knee was absolutely

throbbing, but he was more worried about his wings. He'd been careful to fold them flat against his back as soon as he realized that what he'd taken for the perfect hiding place was, in fact, a tangle of brambles, but he could easily have torn them on the way through.

Although Flower Fairies can't fly that far, their delicate wings are very important to them: as part of their overall camouflage, for balance, and—of course—for flitting from plant to plant and up into trees to visit their friends. Cautiously, Strawberry opened his pair—which resembled pale green petals—and craned his neck round to investigate.

They *looked* all right. He flapped them several times. *Yup, working nicely.*

Next, he straightened his floppy green sunhat and brushed the dirt off his matching red shirt and shorts. Then, feeling satisfied that all was in order, he sat down to attend to his knee.

A big rip in his right stocking revealed a nasty cut. When Strawberry had made sure that he was safely out of sight from the humans, he'd stopped in the middle of the bush and, gritting his teeth, pulled out a large splinter. It hurt a lot, but he was too angry to cry and besides, he couldn't afford to make any more noise having been lucky enough to get away with a yelp of pain already.

"That was *so* stupid," the little Flower Fairy said aloud.

Strawberry had been out exploring the lane when he'd stumbled across a handful of discarded cherry stones. He could never resist a game of fairy marbles and having hollowed out a pit with a stick and selected his shooter, he was soon absorbed in trying to knock the remaining stones into the hole. And because he was concentrating so hard on perfecting his shot, he didn't hear the children until they were almost upon him. So, by the time he'd come to his senses, he had to flee for the nearest cover—which, rather than being a nice safe hedgerow, had turned out to be a very prickly bush. The humans had passed by without noticing him, but Strawberry knew that he'd had a narrow escape and his heart was still thumping, not least because he'd broken one of the first Flower Fairy rules and let his guard slip.

"You could have been trampled on or ... or ... worse still, they might have actually seen you—and then what? Either you'd be imprisoned in one of those glass jar things by now or they'd be searching high and low for the rest of the Flower Fairies and that would all be YOUR FAULT!" Strawberry continued to scold himself as he pulled a handkerchief out of the pocket of his shorts, folded it lengthways and attempted to tie it round his leg.

Just then, he heard what sounded like a giggle and, dropping the makeshift bandage, he jumped to his feet. "Who's there?" he said, looking about but not seeing anyone.

This time there was a snort of laughter— and it came, quite clearly, from the bramble bush. Ignoring the pain in his knee, Strawberry spun round and stood with his hands on his hips. "Show yourself!" he demanded—feeling rather indignant that someone should be laughing at his obvious discomfort.

"I'm not hiding from you, you know," said a voice. "I'm right in front of your nose."

Not quite believing

that anyone would be in among the prickles
out of choice, Strawberry moved closer to
the bush, being careful not to catch himself
on any of the harmful canes. And there,
sitting casually *astride* one of the branches,
was another Flower Fairy!

Strawberry was somewhat taken aback and
stood staring at her for a moment or two. She
had lovely opaque wings that complimented
her soft pink petal skirt and deep purple
tank top. She was grinning at him playfully
and he could see immediately that she

hadn't meant to be unkind. But what
was most surprising was
that her legs and arms
were quite bare and
completely without a
single scratch.

"Boo!" the Flower
Fairy said suddenly,

bringing Strawberry to his senses.

"Sorry—I didn't mean to stare—but . . . but . . . how come . . ."

"How come the thorns don't hurt me?" Finishing his sentence for him, she leapt out of the bush and landed lightly on the ground beside him. "Because it's a blackberry bush and it's my plant so I'm protected," she explained, drawing his attention to the pinkish-white flowers that peeped out of the brambles. Each one had five flat petals and a center made up of lots of hairy yellow stamen—not dissimilar to Strawberry's own flowers.

"Ah," he said, "so you're Blackberry. I think we might be second cousins, you know."

"I think you're right," Blackberry replied. "It's Strawberry, isn't it?" Then without giving him a moment to reply, she linked her

arm in his. "I'm terribly sorry about your knee. Listen, we'll go and visit Self-Heal and she'll patch you up and then perhaps we can come back here for a cup of my special tea or a game of hopscotch? Oh, but your knee probably hurts too much for that ..."

And after stuffing his handkerchief into her own pocket, she led him off down the field, chatting away cheerfully as though they'd been friends forever.

Chapter Two
Happy Days

"Look out—here I come!"

Blackberry, clinging on to a bouncy
weeping willow branch, sprang off the
grassy verge and swung out across
the pool, dipping her toes into
the cool water and whooping
with delight as she went.

Strawberry was
sitting on the
opposite bank,
tugging off his
socks and
shoes. He
grinned
at his
friend as

she gathered
momentum and
soared back and
forth through
the air.

It had been a
couple of weeks
now since she had
taken him to have his
knee bathed and bound by Self-
Heal and, in that time, not only had the cut
completely healed, but he and Blackberry
had become inseparable. It turned out that
they had loads in common—they both liked
playing marbles and hopscotch, teaching the
baby Flower Fairies to roll and crawl, eating
Candytuft's delicious fairy fudge—and
basically anything else that involved having
fun. Sometimes they just lay on their backs
for hours in the open fields watching larks

swooping or clouds skudding across the sky, talking about all the things they'd like to do and see together. And they were constantly finding new ways to make each other laugh.

"Here I go!" Strawberry shouted, grabbing a branch and taking a running jump to launch himself across the pool.

Blackberry had almost come to a standstill, enjoying the sensation of gently swaying with the tree as its branches skimmed across the water. As he passed her by, Strawberry suddenly had an idea. "Watch this," he called. And then taking hold of the branch above his head, he began shinning up it until he'd disappeared into the thick canopy of leaves. Then, bringing his knees up to his chest, he let go of the willow and dive bombed into the lagoon below.

* * *

"There's one!" exclaimed Blackberry, pointing at the fish that darted out of the shadows. It was small with a dark back, golden belly and sides, and beautiful bright red fins.

The two Flower Fairies were lying on the bank on their tummies—minnow-spotting. It was the time of year when male minnows' scales transformed from dull green and black into spectacular colors.

Strawberry loved watching the lively little fish and it was ideal for passing the time while they dried off in the heat of the afternoon sun. Blackberry,

every bit as daring as her friend,
had jumped straight in after him
and soon they were clambering
in and out of the pool, splashing
about and shrieking with
laughter, not stopping until
they had thoroughly exhausted
themselves.

Now, they were so engrossed
in their current activity that
they didn't notice Willow
alight on the grass beside them.
She'd been at the fairy market all
morning and so this was the first
she'd seen of the companions.

"You two are like peas in a pod!" she
exclaimed, gazing at their reflections
in the water, which acted as a mirror now
that the ripples had vanished along with the
minnow.

It was true—both Strawberry and Blackberry had curly dark hair and heart-shaped faces with plump rosy cheeks. Not only were their personalities similar but they looked alike too!

They turned round at once and smiled up at the pretty Flower Fairy. She had long wavy honey-blonde hair and she wore a lovely dress made from the elegant leaves from her tree and stitched with a red ribbon. Her wings were narrow and elongated and almost identical to those of a dragonfly.

"Willow—we've had such a great time swinging from your branches and swimming in the pool!" Blackberry gushed.

"I'm so glad." Willow raised an eyebrow but smiled kindly. "Listen—I've got some warm seed cakes in my basket. You must be ravenous after all that exercise—why don't you join me for tea?"

"Oh, I'd love to—thanks," said Strawberry, 'but it's time I was getting back. The humans have got a new kitten and he's causing havoc in the flower beds—so a garden meeting has been called. Another time, though."

Unwillingly, he got to his feet and prepared to set off. The smell of Willow's freshly-baked cakes was making his mouth water.

"Here you are—one for the road!" Willow laughed as she reached into her basket and handed him a warm little package.

Strawberry grinned and waved goodbye to them both, before heading off towards the

Flower Fairies' Garden and his own special patch, munching happily as he walked.

"Meet me after breakfast in the usual place," Blackberry called after him. Strawberry waved an arm in the air in response. Then, swallowing the last delicious mouthful of honey-coated seeds, he sighed contentedly to himself. Life was good.

Chapter Three
A Revelation

Strawberry shifted impatiently from foot to foot. He was waiting for Blackberry on the lane-side of the garden wall, just as he had done every day for the past fortnight. But today was different. When he'd opened his eyes first thing that morning, he'd been greeted by a very exciting sight. Now he was bursting to tell his friend the news.

It was the first week of June and

summer was well under way. Each day felt hotter than the previous one and as the sun seemed reluctant to go to bed, the evenings were gloriously long. This was when strawberry plants everywhere produced yellowy-green heart-shaped fruit that ripened into soft, juicy, red berries. And for Strawberry, this meant that he'd be hard at work on his patch during the course of the next couple of months.

All the Flower Fairies loved his fruit, but not least Queen of the Meadow—and so whenever he wasn't busy harvesting the berries and carefully storing them, Strawberry would make special trips to the marsh to deliver the pick of the crop to the royal court. It was an industrious period and didn't leave much time for fun, but Strawberry—like all the Flower Fairies— got an enormous amount of pleasure out of tending his plants. He was just thinking about how he would make an extra-large batch of jam this year and give some to all of his friends, including Blackberry, when a familiar voice broke into his thoughts.

"Morning!"

It was Blackberry, at last, skipping down the lane towards him.

"You look very perky—what have you got planned for today?" she asked.

"Hopefully the same as you," Strawberry replied. Then, not able to hold it in any longer, he blurted out, "My first batch of berries has ripened! It's officially the start of the strawberry season—isn't it exciting?"

Blackberry nodded slowly. "Er . . . yes," she said, rather half-heartedly. "But doesn't that mean you've got to spend the day looking after them?"

"Well, yes, of course!" Strawberry looked

slightly confused. "But I've worked it all out. Presumably yours are ripe too—or nearly there? And so we can help each other out and still spend loads of time together. It'll be brilliant."

He grinned broadly at his friend, expecting her to be bubbling over with excitement too. Instead, he couldn't help noticing that she looked really quite sad. "What on earth is the matter?" he asked her.

"Oh, Strawberry—didn't you know—

blackberries aren't ripe until August at the earliest. They're an autumnal fruit, not a summer fruit." And with that, a single tear slid down her cheek.

The little Garden Fairy's face fell. He couldn't believe his ears. "But . . . but . . . I thought *everything* about us was the same."

"So did I," Blackberry responded, sniffing noisily.

They stood in silence for a moment or two, neither of them knowing what to do. Then, all of a sudden, Blackberry said, "This is ridiculous! You're my dearest friend and you always will be and we're not going to let something as silly as this get in the way." She rubbed her eyes furiously and put on her best smile. "Listen—I'm not going to be busy and so there's no reason why I can't come and help you out each day. And then you can come and help me when it's my fruit's turn. It'll be perfect!"

"I hadn't thought of that . . ." Strawberry murmured, immediately feeling much better. He reached over and patted her arm appreciatively. "Well, if you're sure?"

Blackberry nodded enthusiastically.

"Great!" Strawberry said, turning in the direction of the old stone wall. "Come and have a look then and we can decide where to start." And beckoning for her to follow,

he found himself a hand-hold and began to hoist himself up.

* * *

"That should do it." Strawberry said, crawling backwards out from under one of his plants.

He'd been busy placing wet straw all around the patch so that the fruit wouldn't dry out, and he was pleased to have

completed the task before the afternoon sun set in. Glancing up at his friend, he noticed that she looked hot and a little upset.

It was a week now since Blackberry had promised to come and help him each day and she had been as good as her word. She had worked hard alongside him, but now Strawberry could tell that the adventurous Flower Fairy was getting bored.

"I tell you what—let's go for a swim," he suggested suddenly.

"Really?" said Blackberry, brightening up, "but didn't you want to gather a basket of berries today for Queen of the Meadow?"

"It can wait and I could do with a break," Strawberry replied cheerfully. "Besides,

when it's this hot, they spoil
quickly if you pick them."

"Let's go, then,"
Blackberry said eagerly.
"Race you to the willow
pond!"

* * *

"... five, four, three, two, ONE. Ready or
not, here I come!" Strawberry shouted.

The two Flower Fairies were playing a
game of hide-and-seek on their way back to
the garden. The refreshingly cool water had
been the perfect remedy and it was great to
spend some time together, having fun.

"I bet she's hiding somewhere in my
patch," Strawberry said to himself. "I'll be
as quiet as I can and creep up on her." He
chuckled to himself as he took off. They'd
just scrambled over the wall, so it wasn't far
to fly now, plus approaching from the air

would give him a better view. But he'd only flown a short distance and hadn't even begun searching for his friend, when he heard what sounded like a wail of misery.

His stomach lurched—if he wasn't mistaken, it had come from his corner of the garden. Beating his wings as hard as he could, he headed straight for the strawberry patch.

Sure enough, standing there and wringing her hands was Blackberry. She was staring ahead with an expression of utter dismay. "Oh goodness! Oh goodness!" she was saying over and over again. And

when Strawberry followed her gaze, his heart sank right down into his shoes.

It was the most awful scene that he had ever laid eyes on: for strewn all over the place were strands of straw, tattered leaves and squashed berries.

Chapter Four
From Bad to Worse

During the course of the last three days, Strawberry had finally got his patch back in order and a new crop of berries was already ripening. Lots of the Flower Fairies had stopped by to offer their help, bringing him lemonade or something to eat. But he was still feeling miserable.

Everyone agreed that it must have been the kitten who'd made such a mess. Yet no one had been able to come up with a satisfactory solution. So Strawberry had spent every waking minute guarding his plot and, at night, in order to catch a few hours' sleep, he'd liberally sprinkled fairy dust over the plants to cast a spell that would protect them. But his supplies were running low and there was no time to grind up pollen to make some more. Besides, it wasn't a long-term answer to the problem—for him or any of the Garden Fairies.

However, what was bothering him most of all was that he had barely seen Blackberry since the catastrophe had happened. She'd been so helpful at the time, finding other fairies to help clean up, and fetching a cup of calming

camomile tea. She'd even offered to keep watch for the night so that he could get some sleep. But since then she'd only stopped by once and that was just a fleeting visit.

Strawberry blamed himself—she'd been in the middle of telling him a joke, when he'd snapped at her and told her that he was busy. And now he felt guilty because she was just being her usual bubbly self and couldn't know that he didn't feel like laughing. More than that, he missed her. Their last swim together felt like a distant memory now.

The little Flower Fairy was standing in between a row of plants, all of this going through his mind and causing his forehead to wrinkle with concern, when a voice called out.

"Hello there, Strawberry! You'd better watch out or the wind might change and your face will be stuck like that forever!"

It was Herb Robert, grinning at him cheekily. He was a friendly fairy and Strawberry was always pleased to see him. His tiny flower made its home in the nooks and crannies of the wall that bordered the lane, and he was often popping over either to visit his cousin, Geranium, or to catch up on the garden gossip.

"So I hear that all is not well in the Flower Fairies' Garden," Herb Robert said. He was not much taller than Strawberry but his appearance was quite different. He had an angular face with very pointed ears and his wings were those of a brown and pink patterned butterfly.

"Blackberry told me all about it," he went on. "You know, you should go and see Self-Heal—she's full of good ideas. I bet she'd know what to do about this kitten."

Strawberry didn't fully take in this last part—his ears had pricked up at the mention of his friend. "You've been talking to Blackberry? How is she?"

"Well, you'll soon see for yourself," replied Herb Robert. "I believe she's coming to visit you this afternoon. Anyway, I've got to be on my way. Geranium's expecting me for lunch, so I'd better not be late." And without further ado, he waved goodbye and strode off in the direction of the flowerbeds.

Strawberry was surprised at just how
nervous he felt. Once he'd finished watering
his plants and had checked that the kitten
wasn't nearby, he set about straightening
himself up.

He was just pulling on a clean pair of
shoes when a hand came out of nowhere
and covered his eyes.

Then a chirpy voice said, "Guess who?"

"Blackberry!" he exclaimed, his heart lifting for the first time in days.

"Yes, it's me!" she replied, removing her hand from his face.

Strawberry eagerly spun round to greet her. But when he saw that Blackberry hadn't come alone, a huge wave of disappointment washed over him. Next to her stood a slender Flower Fairy dressed in a burgundy and maroon tunic, with gossamer pink wings and a headdress of round purple berries.

"This is Elderberry," his friend said. Strawberry nodded a hello.

"She lives near me and we met the other day," babbled Blackberry. "We had such an adventure—"

"Aren't your berries ripe yet either?" Strawberry butted in, addressing the newcomer rather abruptly.

"No, no. My fruit is autumnal." Elderberry

smiled sweetly. "These ones are dried," she added, touching the crown of berries nestling in her hair.

"Oh," said Strawberry, glancing down, not able to look either of them in the face.

He knew that he should apologize to Blackberry for rudely interrupting her. And he was well aware that he was behaving badly and quite unlike himself. But he had been overcome by an emotion that he had never experienced before and he couldn't seem to help himself. He was jealous.

"Well," said Blackberry, after a moment in which no one had spoken, "Er—I can see that you're busy, so we'll leave you to it."

Strawberry continued to stare at his shoes. There was a gnawing feeling in the pit of his stomach and he felt sick.

"I'll see you—soon?" she added then turned to go, followed by Elderberry, who was obviously puzzled by the friends' odd behavior.

"Bye," Strawberry whispered as he watched the two fairies go flitting off back toward the garden wall.

He stood in the same spot until they were out of sight and then threw himself down to the ground and buried his head in his arms. If he'd been miserable before Blackberry's visit, now he was really wretched.

Chapter Five

Some Wise Words

Of all the Flower Fairies, Self-Heal most resembled a human. Obviously she had wings; she was less than four inches tall and, like many of her friends, pinned her hair back on either side with one of her flowers. But her clothes were more conventional than the other fairies'—she wore an apron over a dress with a waist and puff sleeves, and she had a maternal way about her. More than that, she seemed to possess knowledge outside the ordinary realms of Flower Fairyland.

As well as taking care of her own kind, she helped and healed many creatures from the animal kingdom, and even the naughty elves were known to stop by for a cure or some advice. When Strawberry couldn't bear to dwell on his dreadful encounter with Blackberry any more, he had set his mind to resolving the kitten problem and it was then that Herb Robert's words had popped into his head: *you should go and see Self-Heal—she's full of good ideas.*

So now he was perched on a mushroom stool in the shady corner of the meadow

where Self-Heal lived, watching her bind a field mouse's paw. It struck him that it was quite a novelty these days, to be sitting down and relaxing. Feeling confident that Tulip would be keeping a close eye on his patch, Strawberry cleared his thoughts and enjoyed listening to the little mouse as he chattered away to Self-Heal. "There we are," the gentle Flower Fairy said eventually, as she tied a double-bow to secure the bandage and patted her patient on the head. "Come back in a couple of days and I'll see how it's doing."

After the mouse had squeaked his goodbye and she'd watched him hobble off through the

long grass, Self-Heal turned to Strawberry.
"Well, I don't know about you," she said,
"but I'd love a cup of tea!"

Strawberry sighed and then took a large
thirst-quenching mouthful of mint tea. He
had been talking for a long time now and
although nothing had changed, he somehow
felt different. He had only intended to tell

Self-Heal about the kitten problem but
when she had asked him to start from the
beginning, he found himself relaying all the
events of the last month—from when he had
first met Blackberry, to earlier that afternoon
when he had been so rude to her.

Self-Heal had looked very thoughtful all
the way through his story and then, without
saying a word, she'd sprung to her feet and
begun rifling through her
walnut chest.

"Here we
are—I've
got just the
thing."
She held
out a
small
packet
for

Strawberry to take. "Careful how you open it," she added.

Laying it flat on the ground, he slowly unfolded the beech leaf to reveal a heap of miniscule seeds. "What are these?" he asked curiously.

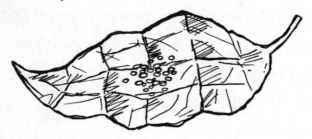

"Cat mint seeds!" Self-Heal replied. "Mix them with some fairy dust to make them grow quickly and sprinkle them all over the Flower Fairies' Garden. It's very important that you choose spots away from everyone's plants to sow them, but I guarantee that before you know it, that kitten won't be causing any more trouble."

"Well, that would be marvelous," said Strawberry, "but how does it work?"

"It's a type of mint that cats can't resist—hence its name," the knowledgeable Flower Fairy explained. "You just watch that kitten of yours. He'll be so busy rubbing up against it, licking and chewing the leaves and purring contentedly that he won't be in the slightest bit interested in anything else in the garden."

"How amazing!" Strawberry exclaimed. "Oh, Self-Heal, you're incredible." And quite forgetting himself, he ran over and gave her an enormous hug.

Self-Heal laughed and then holding
the little Garden Fairy at arm's length, she
looked at him seriously. "As for your other
problem—the only way to solve that is to do
some growing *yourself*."

"What do you mean?" Strawberry was
confused.

"You have to realize that just
because Blackberry has other
good friends, it doesn't
change how she feels
about you. In fact,
it's a good thing."
She paused for
a moment. "It's
great when you
have lots in
common with
someone, but
differences are

important too and so is time apart. It all enriches your friendship and means that the time you have together is even more special. Do you understand?"

"I think so," Strawberry said slowly. It was a lot to think about.

"Good," Self-Heal said, her lovely face breaking into an enormous smile. "Now, run along— you've got some gardening to do!"

* * *

"Fairy dust, fairy dust, make these plants grow—help them spread evenly and not at all slow!"

Strawberry spoke softly, repeating the rhyme as he stirred the special mixture with his forefinger.

Then, taking a good-sized pinch, he flung it out across the lawn. At first, it looked as though the seeds were going to plummet

down and land in the grass, which would
have been disastrous. But then the tiny
particles began to glimmer and sparkle
and gradually they separated
before whizzing off in
various directions
and vanishing
from sight as they
nestled into the
earth.
"Right," said
Strawberry. "With
a little bit of luck, that
will have done the trick.
Now, I'd better let Tulip know
that I'm back and see if I can persuade her to
do another shift for me tomorrow morning,
Although goodness knows if Blackberry
will ever want to talk to me again . . ."

Chapter Six
A Big Surprise

Blackberry was standing on the path next to Elderberry, their heads together as if the two of them were carefully examining something. They looked so at ease with one another that Strawberry couldn't help feeling a pang of jealousy.

"Now," he said under his breath, "remember everything that Self-Heal told you." He took a moment to reflect on her wise words and remind himself how much sense they'd made when he'd mulled them over on the way home. And as he was

thinking about all of this, a terrible notion
came into his head . . . If he didn't stop being
jealous and start behaving like a proper
Flower Fairy, then Blackberry might not
want to be friends with him at all. He gulped.
That would be just too awful.

So, taking a deep breath, he leaned over
and tapped his friend on the shoulder.

Blackberry turned her head and, although
it was just for a second, Strawberry distinctly
saw her eyes light up. His heart filled with
hope.

"Hello." He cleared his throat. "I've come to apologize."

"Apologize?" Blackberry repeated the word, as if she couldn't quite believe her ears.

"Yes," Strawberry replied sheepishly.

By now, Blackberry was on her feet. She shot her friend a glance and Elderberry nodded ever so slightly before disappearing into the meadow grass, stooping to pick up a

long thin object on her way.

The two remaining Flower Fairies stood facing one another, both feeling awkward and neither of them speaking for a moment or two.

"I'm sorry!" Strawberry said suddenly.

"So am I," chimed in Blackberry. "But you go first." She smiled at him, which was enough to give him all the encouragement

that he needed.

"It's like this . . ." And Strawberry went on to explain that he'd only been so unpleasant because he'd missed her so much—and, so, when she did turn up but with another friend, it had made him feel horribly jealous.

Blackberry let out a giggle.

"What's so funny?" he asked, slightly hurt.

"Oh, I'm just so relieved," she said. "I thought you were acting like that because you blamed me for all those plants being destroyed."

"What?" Strawberry replied, as it dawned on him what a huge misunderstanding the whole thing had been.

"Well, I know that you only suggested going for a swim to be nice, and that if it wasn't for me, you'd never have left your patch that day. Besides, when I came back to see you the next morning, you snapped at me." She raised her eyebrows at him as if to emphasize her point.

"Oh, Blackberry. Don't be ridiculous.

I was just upset because there was so much work to do. I really am sorry."

"That's OK!" She caught him round the neck and planted a big kiss on his cheek. "It's so good to see you again!"

Strawberry felt himself blushing to the roots of his hair. But he didn't care. All that mattered was that he and Blackberry were friends again. And from now on, he was always going to let her know exactly what he was feeling so that there weren't any more

silly mix-ups.

* * *

All around the garden small, dense plants with mauve-colored flowers had sprung up overnight, and the kitten couldn't get enough of them.

"Self-Heal is so clever, isn't she?" commented Blackberry to her two friends.

"I know, it's incredible," replied Strawberry, as he watched the cat take another swipe at a clump and then roll over

on to the grass with pleasure.

"It must be such a relief for you all,"
Elderberry said kindly, as she rose to her
feet.

The Garden Fairy nodded in response. It
was true—it would mean that he wouldn't
have to be tied to his patch all the time and
could afford to enjoy himself a bit. "Are you
leaving already?" he asked.

"Yes. I said I'd drop in on
Rose while I was here." The
elegant Flower Fairy
opened her wings in
preparation. Then,
reaching into the
bag at her side,
she pulled out a
familiar-looking
object and held it
out to Strawberry.

"This is for you," she said.

He had only caught a glimpse of it in the meadow, but he knew it was the thing that she had picked up before she'd left him and Blackberry to talk. It was a whistle!

"It's made from a stem from my tree. From what I've seen they play quite well!" Elderberry chuckled.

Strawberry was speechless. Then he said solemnly, "I don't really deserve this—but thank you very much. It's wonderful." He beamed at the Tree Fairy, who winked to show him there were no hard feelings. She tousled Blackberry's hair affectionately, and then flew off in the direction of the rose garden.

"That was the

adventure I tried to tell you about before you were so rude," Blackberry said, digging her friend playfully in the ribs, before she went on. "We spied some boys making them one day. They bored holes in the hollowed-out stems and then played them just like whistles. We thought it might be a nice thing for you to do at the end of a hard day's work."

"Well, you're very thoughtful." Strawberry blushed with pleasure. "And listen—I'll get Ragged Robin to teach me. He's really good at the pipes and I know you'll like him."

As he had this idea, he was struck by the realization that both he and Blackberry were going to benefit greatly from the fact that their fruit ripened at different times of year. He could get to know her autumnal friends and she could meet the Flower Fairies whose plants were in season at the same time as his.

"I'll come and play for you and Elderberry

while you're busy harvesting,' he added, thinking out loud.

"Great!" said Blackberry enthusiastically. 'And don't forget that we'll still have two whole seasons to look forward to when neither of us will be working. We can spend all the time in the world together then. You'll be quite sick of me by the end of next spring!'

"Never!" Strawberry replied.

And he meant it. He knew that he couldn't possibly tire of his outgoing, brilliant companion, but that, also, he'd never let jealousy get in the way of their friendship ever again. Life was too short and there were far too many adventures to be shared!

Visit our Flower Fairies website at:

www.flowerfairies.com

There are lots of fun Flower Fairy games and activities for you to play, plus you can find out more about all your favorite fairy friends!

Log onto the Flower Fairies Friendship Ring

Visit the Flower Fairies website to sign up for the new Flower Fairies Friendship Ring!

★ No membership fee
★ News and updates
★ Every new friend receives a special gift!
(while supplies last)

More tales from these Flower Fairies™ coming soon!

Poppy

Sweet Pea

Jasmine

Willow